Puppy Friends #3

Spot the Sporty Puppy

by Jenny Dale

Illustrated by Frank Rodgers

Storybook

Aladdin Paperbacks

New York   London   Toronto   Sydney   Singapore

Look for these PUPPY FRIENDS books!

#1 *Gus the Greedy Puppy*
#2 *Lily the Lost Puppy*
#3 *Spot the Sporty Puppy*

Coming soon

#4 *Lenny the Lazy Puppy*

First Aladdin Paperbacks edition March 2000

Text copyright © 1999 by Working Partners Limited
Illustrations copyright © 1999 by Frank Rodgers
Activity Fun Pages text copyright © 2000 by Stasia Ward Kehoe
First published 1999 by Macmillan Children's Books U.K.
Created by Working Partners Limited

Aladdin Paperbacks
An imprint of Simon & Schuster
Children's Publishing Division
1230 Avenue of the Americas
New York, NY 10020

Library of Congress Catalog Card Number: 99-67699
ISBN 0-689-83424-1

Reprinted by arrangement with Aladdin Paperbacks,
an imprint of Simon & Schuster Children's Publishing Division.

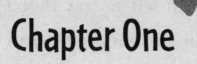

Chapter One

"Fetch the ball, Spot!"

Spot went chasing across the field. He grabbed the squeaky ball in his teeth and raced back to Matt. The ball made a dreadful noise as he ran.

"Good boy, Spot!" Matt, Spot's owner, knelt down and stroked his Dalmatian puppy's silky black ears. "You're a really fast runner!"

Spot wagged his tail proudly and licked Matt's hand. Spot loved running nearly as much as he loved Matt. He would put his ears back and race from one end of the field to the other, feeling the wind rushing past him and ruffling his fur. It was better than a big, juicy bone, or even a roll in a dirty puddle.

Matt looked at his watch. "Time to go home, Spot, or I'm going to be late for school."

Spot whined grumpily. He didn't want to go home yet. Every morning Matt took him for a long walk in the playing field behind their house, where Spot met up with some of the other dogs that lived in their street. They usually had races, and

Spot, of course, always won. But this morning Matt seemed in a hurry.

"Sorry, Spot," Matt said as he clipped the leash to his puppy's collar. "I promise I'll take you out for a longer walk tonight."

Spot woofed. He didn't really mind going home, because he had a special secret. A *very* special secret. When Matt was at school and Mrs. Robinson, Matt's mom, was at work, Spot could run around the field as much as he liked!

Matt and Spot went across the field to the Robinsons' backyard.

Matt opened the gate and then closed it carefully behind them. "Come on, Spot! Race you to the kitchen!"

Spot dashed through the yard, his white tail wagging furiously from side to side, and got to the open kitchen door just before Matt did. He dived into the kitchen and skidded across the floor, stopping with expert timing in front of his empty bowl.

"You're just in time for breakfast, Spot!" laughed Mrs. Robinson, who was spreading butter on toast. She shook some dog food into the bowl, and Spot began to crunch noisily.

"You won, Spot!" Matt said with a grin. "Mom, did you wash my gym clothes for Field Day this afternoon?"

Spot stopped eating and pricked up his ears. Did Matt say *Field Day?*

Matt saw Spot looking eagerly up at him and smiled. "I know, I know you'd love a 'Spot's Field Day.'"

Spot barked in agreement. But he didn't know what this Field Day was, so he wasn't very interested. He went back to eating.

"You *are* coming to watch, aren't you, Mom?" Matt asked.

Mrs. Robinson nodded. "I'll be home from work at lunchtime, so I'll be there to cheer you on."

"Great!" said Matt. "I'm going to try really hard to win one of the races this year!"

Spot's ears pricked up again when he heard the word *race*. He still didn't know what Field Day was, but he was beginning to like the sound of it! He hoped that he would be allowed to go this afternoon, too.

"Time to go, Matt," said Mrs. Robinson.

Spot dashed over to the kitchen door and barked.

"Do you want to stay in the yard this morning, Spot?" asked Mrs. Robinson with a smile.

Spot barked again, so she carried the puppy's bowls outside and gave

6

him some more food and some fresh water. "Matt, did you shut the back gate?" she asked. "We don't want Spot getting out."

Matt nodded. "Bye, Spot. See you later."

Spot waited until he heard the car start up and drive away, taking Mrs. Robinson to work and Matt to school. Then he scampered eagerly to the other end of the garden. He scrabbled about at the bottom of the hedge and uncovered his secret: a small hole. He squeezed his way through, and then he was out in the playing field again.

Spot ran joyfully across the grass, sniffing the air as he went. He knew he wasn't really allowed out on his own, but he got so bored at home when Matt was at school. This way he could meet up with all his other friends!

He ran about on his own for a while, scrabbling in the hedges and finding lots of interesting smells. Then he saw Jasper the black Labrador, who lived a few doors away from the Robinsons. Jasper was out with his owner, Mr. Smith.

Spot bounded up to him and gave him a friendly nudge with his nose. "Come on, I'll race you to the other end of the field!" he barked.

"Oh no, not again!" Jasper groaned. "You always beat me!"

"Hello, Spot." Mr. Smith bent down and patted the dalmatian. "You're out on your own again, I see!"

Spot woofed and wagged his tail. He hoped Mr. Smith wouldn't say anything to the Robinsons, or his special secret would be discovered!

Spot and Jasper set off across the field. Spot was soon in front and he won the race easily, before Jasper had even run halfway. The Labrador gave up, panting.

"You shouldn't eat so many biscuits!" Spot yapped at him. "Then you'd be able to run as fast as me!"

Jasper lay down and put his nose between his paws. "I need a rest!" he whined.

Spot suddenly thought of something. "Jasper, do you know what 'Field Day' is?"

"It's a special day for children at school," Jasper woofed back. "They have lots of races, and all the moms and dads go to watch."

Spot's eyes lit up. A moment later he

was running away across the field again.

"Where are you going?" Jasper barked after him.

"Home!" Spot barked back. "I don't want to miss Field Day!"

It seemed a very long time to Spot before Mrs. Robinson arrived home at lunchtime. He jumped around, whining impatiently, as she opened the back door.

"Hello, Spot!" She patted him, then checked that he still had water in his bowl. "I've got to rush—I'm late for Field Day!"

Spot began to bark at the top of his voice, feeling very excited. He could hardly wait to go join in all the races!

"No, you can't come, I'm afraid, Spot," said Matt's mom, and she quickly locked the back door again.

Spot slumped miserably on the grass. *Why* couldn't he go to Field Day? After all, he was the fastest dog on the street! If there were races going on, he ought to be allowed to take part in them. . . .

Spot's ears pricked up. He could hear voices. Lots of them. It sounded as if there were suddenly lots of people in the playing field.

He hurried down to the end of the yard and looked through his secret hole in the hedge.

There *were* lots of people in the field. And there were some strange, exciting things happening, too. Balloons and streamers had been tied up in the trees. There were lots of chairs laid out in rows, as well as a small platform with people standing on it.

Spot was puzzled. Who were all these people, and what was going on?

Then, to his delight, Spot saw Matt! The puppy could hardly believe his eyes. So *this* must be Field Day! And it was happening right there, on his own playing field! Spot only had to squeeze through the secret hole to go join in the fun. And that was just what he was going to do!

Chapter Two

Spot was so excited, it took him a moment or two to wriggle his way through the hole in the hedge. But at last, he did it. He raced happily across the field toward the crowd of people, hoping he hadn't missed any of the races. But nothing much seemed to be happening, except that a man was standing on the little platform, talking to the parents and children who sat in rows on either side of him.

". . . And as principal of Redhill Elementary School, it gives me great pleasure to welcome all of you here to Field Day," the man was saying. "We'll start with the special teachers' race. All the teachers will be taking part, including myself!"

Spot had heard Matt talking about the principal. His name was Mr. Brown, and Matt was a bit scared of him because he was very strict. As people clapped after the principal's speech, Spot bared his teeth and growled a little. He hoped Mr. Brown didn't win!

Nobody noticed the puppy as he looked around for Matt. The teachers were lining up at the top of the track for the start of the race. There were two children standing at the bottom end, holding a tape stretched out between them. That was the finish line.

Spot felt very excited. How wonderful it would feel to be the first to cross the line and win! All these people would jump up and cheer, and Matt would be very proud of him. . . .

"Spot! What on earth are *you* doing here?"

Spot's heart sank. Mrs. Robinson had seen him! She had jumped up from her seat and was hurrying across the grass toward him. She didn't look very pleased, either.

Spot knew very well that if he was caught he'd be taken home again, so he scurried off as fast as his legs could carry him.

"Spot, you naughty boy!" Mrs. Robinson called. "Come back!"

Spot pretended he hadn't heard. He decided to find a place to hide and wriggled under a row of chairs, squeezing his way around people's legs.

Some of the people leaned down and tried to grab him as he rushed by. But Spot managed to wriggle away from them.

Just then, Mrs. Williams, the school

secretary, shouted, "On your mark! Get set! *Go!*"

The teachers' race had started! Spot crawled forward to sit under a chair in the front row, right next to the track. He poked his head out to see what was going on.

The teachers were all charging across the grass toward the finish line. Mr.

Brown was in the lead, and he looked determined to win.

Spot wondered if the other teachers were letting Mr. Brown win because he was the principal. He wished *he* had a chance to race against Mr. Brown—he was sure he could beat him.

"Spot!"

That was Matt's voice. Spot sat up eagerly and looked around.

"Spot!"

Then Spot saw his owner. Matt was dressed in his gym clothes and was standing on the opposite side of the track with his best friend, Daniel Parsons.

Spot was so excited, he dashed out from under the chair where he was hiding and across the track. At exactly the same moment the teachers came running at full speed toward him, with Mr. Brown still in the lead.

Spot had no time to get out of the way. Neither did the principal. They crashed into each other with a yelp and a shout. Mr. Brown tripped over Spot and went flying head over heels, landing in a heap on the grass!

Chapter Three

"Who . . . what . . . ?" sputtered Mr. Brown in a dazed voice as he pulled himself to his feet. "What is this . . . this *animal* doing here?"

Spot cowered in the grass, feeling very frightened. He hadn't meant to trip Mr. Brown. The principal looked very big and menacing as he towered over

Spot. The puppy was glad when Matt rushed over and picked him up.

"Sorry, sir," Matt said breathlessly. "He's mine."

"And what's he doing at Field Day?" Mr. Brown glared down at Spot, who huddled even closer to Matt. "No dogs are allowed!"

"He must have gotten out of our back-yard somehow," Matt explained quickly. "We live right there." He pointed to his house.

Mr. Brown opened his mouth to say something else, then changed his mind. He'd noticed that some of the children and their parents were laughing, and even the teachers who'd now finished the race were trying not to smile.

"Well, get rid of him, then," he snapped. "And quickly!"

Spot whimpered as Matt hurried across the track toward his mom. The parents and children who were watching were still laughing and pointing at them. Spot felt very ashamed of himself.

"It's OK, Spot," Matt whispered quietly into his puppy's ear. "Thanks to you, my teacher, Miss Marshall, won the race!"

Spot looked up at Matt and gave him a grateful lick on the chin. He felt a bit better now. Then Spot saw the look on Mrs. Robinson's face. . . .

"You're a very bad boy, Spot!" she scolded as Matt handed the puppy to

her. "You could have caused a serious accident!"

Spot whimpered anxiously and tried to lick her hand.

"This is your fault as well, Matt," Mrs. Robinson went on. "You must not have closed the back gate properly this morning, and Spot must have gotten out."

Spot felt terrible when he heard that. He didn't want Matt to be blamed when it wasn't his fault. He began to whine loudly, but stopped as he saw Mr. Brown glaring at him again.

"I'd better take Spot home right away," Mrs. Robinson said, sighing, "before he can do any more damage!"

Matt's face fell. "But if you go now, you'll miss my first race!" he said. "It's the egg and spoon."

Mrs. Robinson hesitated. "Well, all right. I'll stay and watch that first."

Spot's tail began to wag a little. At least he was going to see Matt take part in *one* race!

"You'd better behave yourself now,

Spot," Mrs. Robinson said firmly as she sat down with the puppy on her lap. "I think Mr. Brown's had enough of you for one day!"

"Hello, Spot!" said the woman who was sitting next to Mrs. Robinson.

Spot knew who she was and wagged his tail. It was Mrs. Parsons, Daniel's mom, and she had Daniel's little sister, Emma, in her arms.

"Dog!" said Emma, trying to grab Spot's ear. "Dog! Woof, woof!"

Spot licked her hand, and Emma squealed with delight.

"Look, Emma," said Mrs. Parsons, lifting the little girl up. "There's Daniel and Matt!"

Spot looked up the track too, and saw Matt and his friend lining up for the egg and spoon race. Spot wasn't sure what an egg and spoon race was. Did the children have to eat the egg with the spoon?

"On your marks!" shouted Mr. Brown, who was starting off the race.

Spot was amazed to see that all the children, including Matt, were holding a spoon with an egg balanced on it.

"Get set!" shouted Mr. Brown. "*Go!*"

The race began. The children set off, half-running and half-walking, carefully holding their eggs and spoons in front of them.

Spot watched, puzzled. What a strange race! But he began to get excited when he saw that Matt was in the lead!

"Come on, Matt!" shouted Mrs. Robinson, bouncing Spot up and down on her knee.

Spot barked loudly, straining forward to get a better view. Matt was still in the lead, running along very carefully, his eyes fixed on the egg in front of him.

But then, just as Matt drew level with Mrs. Robinson and Spot, he stumbled. The egg fell off his spoon into the grass.

Matt's mom had gotten so excited watching the race that she'd loosened her grip on Spot. Spot didn't hesitate. He leaped off her lap and dashed across the grass to pick up the egg. If he took it to the finish line, Matt might still win!

The other children taking part in the race were so surprised to see Spot darting in front of them that they all dropped their eggs too. Spot ignored them and grabbed Matt's egg in his teeth.

The egg was surprisingly hard and shiny. It felt more like a stone or a pebble. Spot decided it couldn't be a real egg, after all.

"Spot!" Matt was running toward him. "Come here!"

Spot galloped off toward the finish line, making sure that Matt was following him. He dashed under the tape and was thrilled to hear cheers from the crowd.

Matt followed him a few seconds later. They'd won! Spot danced around Matt's ankles, barking loudly with delight.

"This dog is ruining our Field Day!" boomed an angry voice.

Everyone fell silent as Mr. Brown, panting and red in the face, hurried down the track toward Matt and Spot.

Alarmed, Spot hid behind Matt's legs, trying to make himself as small as possible. He'd done the wrong thing *again*. But he'd only wanted to help Matt win a race!

"I'm terribly sorry, Mr. Brown," said Mrs. Robinson as she rushed over and picked Spot up. "I'll take him home right away."

"Thank you," snapped the principal. "I think we'd better run the race again— and this time we'll do it properly."

Spot looked miserably over Mrs. Robinson's shoulder as she carried him away from all the fun. He'd gotten Matt into trouble again, and they hadn't even won the race in the end. It looked as if Field Day was over for Spot.

Chapter Four

"In you go, Spot." Mrs. Robinson swung open the back gate and took the puppy inside the yard. She frowned. "Why wasn't the gate still open? Oh, well, the wind must have blown it shut after you'd gotten out."

She wagged her finger sternly at Spot.

"Now you behave yourself until we get back!"

Spot sat on the grass and looked up at Mrs. Robinson, his brown eyes miserable.

Mrs. Robinson couldn't help smiling. "It's all right, Spot," she said, giving him a pat. "I know you didn't mean any harm. Be a good boy, now. We'll be home soon."

She went out again, checking the gate to make sure it was properly shut.

Gloomily, Spot lay down and put his nose between his paws. He'd really made a mess of things this time. He'd gotten Matt into trouble with his mom *and* with his principal.

Suddenly the people in the field started cheering loudly. Spot couldn't help himself. He dashed straight over to his secret hole to see what was going on. But he was too far away to see anything much.

Everyone at Field Day was having fun except him, and it didn't seem at all fair that he was left out.

Spot made up his mind and wriggled

through the hole again. This time, he'd keep out of sight. He'd find a quiet hiding place where he could watch the races without being seen.

He crept cautiously across the field, keeping a sharp lookout. Some of the smallest children in the school were having a sack race, and they were all getting tangled up in their sacks and falling over. Everyone was watching the race, so no one noticed Spot at all.

On the grass was a pile of sacks that weren't being used. Spot crawled toward them on his tummy and quickly burrowed his way underneath them.

He lay still for a moment or two, then carefully poked his head out and looked around. He soon dived back under the sacks again, though, because the first thing he saw was Mr. Brown's shoes. The principal was standing right next to him!

"Class 3M! Jump rope race next!" shouted Mr. Brown loudly.

Spot knew that Matt was in Class 3M, so he risked a quick look out from under the sacks again. Luckily Mr. Brown had walked over to the starting line.

Spot had quite a good view, and he was thrilled to see Matt and Daniel lining up next to each other with jump ropes. He longed to bark loudly to encourage Matt, but he didn't dare.

"On your marks!" Mr. Brown boomed

as the entrants stood holding their jump ropes ready. Spot could hardly sit still because he was so excited.

"Get set!"

It was then that Spot noticed little Emma Parsons, Daniel's sister, in the distance. She was toddling along on her own across the field, stopping now and then to pick a daisy.

Spot could see that Emma's mom was talking to Mrs. Robinson. She'd probably put Emma down for a minute and not noticed that she'd wandered off, Spot decided.

Then Spot noticed something else: Emma was heading toward the open gateway at the top of the field.

Spot knew that beyond the gate was a very busy and dangerous road. Out on his leash with Matt, Spot had seen all sorts of huge, scary trucks and buses on that road. Fast cars raced along it too. Spot was sure that little Emma shouldn't go near the road on her own.

"Go!" shouted Mr. Brown.

At the same moment, Spot leaped to his feet and rushed out from under the pile of sacks. He had to stop Emma from going through the gate. But would he make it in time?

Chapter Five

Spot took the quickest route toward Emma—which was straight across the track.

"It's that pest of a dog again!" roared Mr. Brown furiously as Spot suddenly appeared and dashed in front of the skipping children. All of them, including Matt, had to stop quickly, and most of them tripped on their jump ropes and fell.

"Spot!" yelled Matt, trying to untangle himself from his rope. "Spot, come here!"

Spot took no notice. He knew he was a fast runner, but this was the fastest he had ever run in his life.

"Matthew Robinson! Will you get that dog of yours under control!" Mr. Brown was shouting at the top of his voice as he dashed down the track. "I've had just about enough of this!"

"I'm trying, sir!" gasped Matt, who was still trying to untangle himself.

"I want that dog caught and taken away immediately—*Aargh!*" Mr. Brown tripped over a trailing jump rope and fell flat on his face.

"Are you all right, Mr. Brown?" asked Mrs. Robinson, who had hurried out from the audience to help.

"Yes, yes, never mind me!" Mr. Brown muttered furiously as he struggled to his feet. "Just catch that dog!"

"Spot!" shouted Mrs. Robinson. "Come back, right now!"

Spot ignored all the noise behind him and kept going, his eyes fixed firmly on Emma. Suddenly the field seemed very big and very long—and every second was taking Emma closer to the open gate and dangerous road beyond it. Spot wasn't sure he could get there in time, but he knew he had to try.

"Spot!" Matt was racing along behind him, followed by Mrs. Robinson, Mr. Brown, and some of the other teachers who had joined in the chase. "Spot, will you *please* come back?"

Just then, Daniel Parsons noticed something. "Look, Mom!" he shouted.

"Isn't that Emma heading toward the gate?"

"Oh my goodness, so it is!" gasped Mrs. Parsons, her face turning pale. "She must have wandered off!" Mrs. Parsons and Daniel leaped up and ran after the others.

Mr. Brown had noticed Emma, too, and had forgotten about being angry with Spot. "Quick!" he shouted. "That child is heading toward the open gate. She'll be out on the main road any minute!"

"But look, Spot's trying to stop her!" Matt shouted in an excited voice. "Go on, Spot! Good boy! You can do it, I know you can!"

Spot heard Matt's shout from behind him and forced himself to run even faster. His legs were so tired, but Emma was almost at the open gate. Spot knew he had to make an extra big effort now to reach the toddler and somehow stop her from going through it.

Yes! Spot leaped past Emma and swerved to a stop in front of her, making her stop too. By now they were right next to the gate. The sound of trucks and cars racing along outside was deafening.

"Dog!" said Emma happily, having no idea she had been in such danger. She patted the puppy. "Spot!"

Spot barked weakly. He felt as if he had no breath left. He'd just run the most important race of his life—and he'd won!

Chapter Six

"Good boy, Spot!" Matt reached Spot and Emma first. He picked his puppy up and hugged him.

Mrs. Parsons was right behind Matt. She grabbed Emma and gave her a big hug too. "You shouldn't have gone off like that, Emma!" she said tearfully. "But thanks to Spot, you're safe!"

"Spot's a hero!" Daniel added as they walked back to the racetrack. All the children and parents and teachers cheered the puppy.

Only Mr. Brown stayed silent. "Er . . . well," he muttered as everyone turned to look at him. "I think that, er . . . Spot . . . has done very well. Very well indeed. . . . And he's welcome to stay and watch the rest of Field Day. . . . "

Everyone cheered and pretended not to hear when Mr. Brown added, " . . . if he promises to behave himself!"

Spot barked loudly with delight, wagging his tail. He even thought about leaning over to lick Mr. Brown's hand, but he decided against it. Spot still found the principal a bit scary.

Everyone sat down, ready to continue with Field Day. Mrs. Parsons kept a tight hold of Emma's hand.

Mr. Brown announced that they would hold Class 3M's jump rope race again, so Matt had to hurry off.

"I'm really proud of you, Spot!" he whispered in Spot's ear before he handed the puppy over to Mrs. Robinson. "You showed Mr. Brown just what a brilliant dog you are!"

Spot's heart swelled with pride. He sat on Mrs. Robinson's knee to watch the jump rope race, hoping that Matt would win.

Sadly, Matt and Daniel got tangled up in each other's ropes and they both came in last. Spot was a bit disappointed, but this time he didn't try to interfere and stayed quietly on Mrs. Robinson's lap.

It was great fun watching all the different races, and Spot barked loudly through all of them, even the ones Matt wasn't in.

The running race came last, and Spot thought that Matt had a good chance of winning. He sat forward eagerly as children from Class 3M lined up at the top of the track.

Matt waved at him. "I'm going to try to run as fast as you, Spot!" he called.

Spot barked his support, then turned around and licked Mrs. Robinson's chin excitedly.

Mr. Brown got ready to start the race.

"On your marks! Get set! *Go!*" he shouted.

Matt and the others started running. Spot was dismayed to see that at first a tall girl with very long legs was in the lead, but then he saw that Matt was catching up with her.

"Go on, Matt!" he barked. "You can do it!"

Matt heard Spot barking and that made him run even faster. He passed the girl and crossed the finish line—first!

Mrs. Robinson was almost as excited as Spot, and she jumped up and down with the puppy in her arms. "He won, Spot! He won!"

Spot was so proud, he couldn't stop barking. He had been hoping and hoping that Matt would come in first in a race, and now he had!

When the last race was over, it was time for Mr. Brown to present certificates to the winners. Their names were called out one by one, and each winner went up onto the platform to shake hands with the principal.

Spot waited impatiently for Matt's turn. When Matt went up on that platform, Spot was going to bark louder than he'd ever barked in his life!

"And now the Class 3M running race," Mr. Brown announced. Spot's tail began to wag furiously. "Our winner is . . . Matthew Robinson!"

Everyone clapped as Matt went up onto the platform, but they laughed too, because Spot was barking madly.

Mr. Brown gave Matt his certificate, then he turned to the audience. "Field Day is almost over now, but I have one very special presentation to make before we all go home."

Everyone sat up, wondering what was about to happen.

"We have a very clever dog here today," Mr. Brown went on. "And after a few . . . er . . . goof-ups, he has helped to make our Field Day a great success!" The principal went a bit red, then laughed along with everyone else. "So it gives me great pleasure to present a special certificate to Spot Robinson!"

Spot could hardly believe his ears. *He* was going to get a certificate?

"Come here, Spot!" Matt called excitedly. "Come get your certificate!"

Spot didn't need to be told twice. He dived off Mrs. Robinson's knee and raced up onto the platform.

Mr. Brown bent down and patted Spot, then he gave the certificate to Matt.

"Look, Spot!" Matt knelt down and showed him the certificate.

"It says:

For Spot,
the bravest and fastest dog we know.
From all the children and teachers
at Redhill Elementary School.

Everyone cheered and clapped. Spot was so pleased and proud, he couldn't even bark. This time he *did* jump up and lick Mr. Brown's hand!

Mr. Brown smiled and looked quite pleased.

"We'll pin it up in the kitchen, near your bed," Matt said as he gave his puppy a hug. "This really has been *Spot's* Field Day!"

Puppy Friends Activity Fun Pages

Developed by Stasia Ward Kehoe

Sporty Spot Trivia Quiz

1. What is Spot's very special secret?
2. What kind of a dog is Spot?
3. Why is Matt a bit scared of Principal Brown?
4. What kind of race is Matt's first race?
5. Why is Emma in danger?

(see answers at bottom of page)

Puppy Paperweights

Keep a puppy in view with this cool puppy paper-weight while you're doing your homework or surfing the Internet.

You will need:

Two flat rocks (one slightly larger than the other)

Craft glue

Safety scissors

Felt scraps

Small plastic beads, pom-poms, and/or google eyes
    (available at most craft stores)

Answers: 1. When the family is away, Spot can run in the field as much as he likes. 2. A dalmatian 3. Because he is a bit strict. 4. Egg and spoon 5. Because she is walking toward a busy road.

Place the larger rock on your work surface. This rock will be the puppy's body. Glue on the smaller "head" rock. (HINT: You may want to ask an adult to use an ultra-hold glue to attach the rocks.) Allow glue to dry completely. Cut two ears, four paws, and a tail from the felt scraps. Glue them onto the rocks. Select beads for the nose and eyes (or use google eyes). Glue on your puppy's feet and features. Add more details, such as spots or a collar, if desired. Put your finished paperweight on your desk, or give it to a puppy-loving friend.

Name That Pup

It is fun to think of names for pets. Spot probably got his name because of the black spots dalmatians have on their fur. Try thinking up super names for these special animals:

A tiny brown puppy with white paws
An enormous, friendly, all-black dog
A brown-and-white beagle that loves to run and play
A shy, quiet puppy with short white fur
A golden cat with a very long tail
A spunky orange hamster who loves to nibble cardboard

A pair of sleepy gerbils

A supersized goldfish

Try drawing a picture of one of the pets you have named above—or write a story about it!

Super Certificates

It's always nice to get an award for a job well done. Make a certificate for a family member or friend who has done something nice for you: your brother, for not barging into your room all week; your mom, for leaving work early to coach your soccer team; or your friend, for getting a part in the school play.

You will need:

A large sheet of colored paper

A slightly smaller sheet of white paper

Craft scissors

Pen or pencil

Stickers, stamps, or glitter glue

Using the pen, complete the following sentences on the white paper:

SUPER CERTIFICATE!

For _____

Date _____

Signed (your name)_____

Glue the white paper onto the colored paper to create a frame. Decorate you certificate with stickers, stamps, glitter glue, or other craft materials. Choose a special moment to award your certificate.

Puppy Care Pointer

Some dogs need more exercise than others. Do you own a large dog, or a dog from a breed once used for hard work and distance running? Then you will have to make sure it gets daily walks or runs and plenty of fast-paced playtime. Smaller dogs and some guard dogs are naturally less active and require less walking and exercising. Take the time to find out how much exercise your pup really needs—and how much she will need as she grows up—and make keeping her fit part of your daily routine.